T0145035

# MY FRIEND PHILLIP

## CONSCIOUS KIDS

written by Zainab Ansari

illustrations by Farwah Zaidi and Zahra Ansari

Archway Publishing books may be ordered through booksellers or by contacting:

Archway Publishing
1663 Liberty Drive
Bloomington, IN 47403
www.archwaypublishing.com
1 (888) 242-5904

ISBN: 978-1-4808-9142-5 (sc)
ISBN: 978-1-4808-9143-2 (e)

Print information available on the last page.

Archway Publishing rev. date: 6/16/2020

"You presume you are a small entity, but within you is enfolded the entire universe."

My friend Phillip loves to talk. He talks and talks nonstop! When I want eggs for breakfast, he says, "Are you sure you want eggs today? Why don't you have pancakes instead? Actually, pancakes may take too long to make; let's stick to the eggs instead."

My friend Phillip is so full of opinions. He has something to say about everything! When I'm picking out clothes to wear, he says, "Hmmm, do you really want to wear that bright-red shirt? What if everyone laughs at you? Why don't you wear the orange one instead? No, the orange one is too thick; you might get hot. How about you wear a T-shirt instead? What about the one you got for Christmas from your aunt Shelly?" Yikes!

My friend Phillip can get very excited. When he gets worked up about something, he can go on and on and on about it forever. "You shouldn't have worn these shoes today. You should've worn the other ones instead. These ones have laces, and that's why you tripped! You never would have tripped had you been wearing the Velcro shoes. You always do this!"

My friend Phillip sometimes makes things seem much worse than they really are. The night before my first day at my new school, he kept me up almost all night long. He said all kinds things that night: "Nobody is going to like you; everybody is going to laugh at you. Your teacher is going to be mean, and you are going to hate it there. This is all your parents' fault for choosing to move! How could they not think of you? They are so selfish!"

It turns out that my first day at my new school was fantastic! I made lots of new friends, and I loved my teacher. Everybody was so nice to me, and the gymnasium was the biggest I had ever seen. I had wasted an entire night of sleep worrying for no reason and getting mad at my parents for absolutely nothing!

My friend Phillip can be wrong sometimes, but I always end up listening to him anyway.

My friend Phillip can be very distracting. When I am in class trying to concentrate on my work, he says things like, "I wonder if Jake will want to play road hockey this evening. He couldn't play last night because his mom wouldn't let him out. What if the same thing happens tonight? You have no one else to play road hockey with. This will be the second night you won't get to play road hockey. You should make more friends in your neighbourhood who play road hockey."

My friend Phillip is so judgmental. He has opinions about everyone! "Don't talk to her; she seems snobby. She will be nice to your face and then make fun of you behind your back. Don't trust him; he seems like a liar. He will pretend to be your friend and then blame everything on you when he gets in trouble!"

My friend Phillip loves to go down memory lane. He brings up painful memories from the past and makes me cry sometimes. I wish he never, ever brought up those memories.

My friend Phillip always reminds me when I need to be scared. "I wouldn't go near those monkey bars; remember what happened last time? You broke your arm falling from those monkey bars and had to be in a cast for a whole month!" I sometimes wish he would stop bringing up the cast. He scares me out of doing a lot of fun activities with that cast story.

My friend Phillip can get very jealous sometimes. When I didn't make the basketball team and my friend Brian did instead, Phillip went on about it for days. It was the worst time ever! He constantly reminded me that Brian was better and faster and stronger than me and that he was much more athletic and built than I was. Phillip said I could never be like Brian! Why couldn't I be like Brian? Why couldn't I make the team? Is Brian really better than me? Why? I felt horrible!

But the very next year, I tried out for the basketball team again, and I made it! I just had to brush up on a few skills. I wasted an entire year sulking for no reason. Phillip was wrong again.

My friend Phillip never gets tired of talking. He could talk forever and ever about all kinds of things. Most of the time he is very wrong, but he talks and talks anyway.

I have learned to stop paying attention to Phillip. I let him talk and talk, but instead of getting all caught up in everything he says, I just watch him instead. I let him talk, and I watch. I don't get upset, I don't get confused, and I don't get involved. I don't feel indecisive, I don't doubt myself, and I don't get emotional. I don't let Phillip get to me. I just watch.

Sometimes I turn him off completely. I have learned to do that twice a day—once in the morning and once in the evening. This is my quiet time without Phillip. During this time, I get to be myself.

I sit on my bed alone, and for ten minutes I don't allow Phillip to say anything. If he begins talking, I remind myself that this is my time alone and that I want complete silence. In this silence, I am myself.

Each time I do this, I build my awareness, and it grows and grows. This awareness helps me to not get involved in everything he says throughout the day. It allows me to sit on the sidelines and watch instead. Otherwise I might get sad, angry, afraid, worried, nervous, anxious, or jealous for no reason. I don't like feeling any of those things.

Phillip is a build-up of energy within me that needs to be released; the energy creates thoughts inside my head that can cause worry, anxiety, fear, anger, sadness, jealousy, and nervousness. The more you can sit on the sidelines and watch, the smaller and less impactful they become.

We all have a friend like Phillip. These are the hundreds of thoughts we have in a day—the stuff that goes through our mind constantly that we don't say out loud.

Give your thoughts a name and a body. Picture them as a person whom you spend your entire day with. This will help you identify them and separate them from yourself. You are not your thoughts. Your thoughts are just a build-up of energy that needs to be released.

Give yourself some quiet time twice a day, every day. This is very important because in this time, you are your true self, and within you is enfolded the entire universe.

Printed in the United States
By Bookmasters